Hip Hop War

Table of Contents

Introduction

In the 1970's hip hop music started from the urban culture in New York. It was considered an unground music genre at the time. Women in hip hop had a long way to go in gaining the respect of their male counter-parts.

By the late 1990's although there were women in the industry such as: Loren Heal, Salty & Better, Mc Like, Mitzi, Fox Zee, Even, etc. they were not the first to spearhead that genre They all left their unique footprint in the culture.

Who was the first Queen of Rap? Queen Califia played a crucial part in bringing unity to the females emcees. She is the 1st Queen

Lil Keisha aka Queen Be Luv the 1st to unapologetic expressed her sexuality and femininity so explicitly in the male dominated industry. Keisha not only rapped about sex she exudes with confidence throughout her fashion apparel. Her iconic fashions would be a trailblazer throughout the industry and culture for decades to come.

Just a reminder since you have on blinders I'm the first you can't erase if it wasn't for me you would have no place

you've been jocking my style for a while it's on my resume check my file

I'm the blueprint your the indent something was strange then it all change

the end of my reign came like an infection music spreaded in a different direction for what it's worth I gave birth

I lost my connection along with my protection under that umbrella came another era

To differrent races with similar cases so many changing faces with small traces hidden in secret places

I heard you had injuries from to many surgeries unrecognizable a blast from the past pitiful you look like an outcast

Queen of Rap what a mishap you lost the crown and now you handicap

Stuck in the past reminiscing ain't nobody listening while you keep on wishing Ima keep on representing

There's a difference between showing homage and kissing ass I not in school don't need a hall pass

Who was the next Queen? *Re Re the go between held the crown temporary.... Unil she tried to send her friend with Jesus and Mary.*

I came in the ring you know what that means picked up the crown but didn't kiss the ring They all frown cause I'm the Queen now you in your feelings as though it seems It's a competition or you lack comprehension no time for Kumbaya I came in lynching

Who died and made you Queen? Queen Be! **Bonsai died?** *No.... Queen Be Luv music died in 2005*

Why you mad at me? *I enhanced your style to level 3 don't blame me blame the industry*

The only competition from back in the day free Re Re is what
I say Finally came home trying to
reclaim the thrown unfortunately for her
that's where she went wrong

Ebony and Ivory went from friends to rivalries in war there
are causalities add you to my adversaries
Shether was a teacher reminded me of grim
reaper made me a better thinker

could it be a female creature soul ties even
deeper held on like a leacher can't break them
better release her

you was to bitter and eager now you about to meet her
looking for some clarity but at the same time hating me or
self the choices we make are the cards that were dealt

*I hit the decade mark and passed the chart they didn't know
I was a shark*

*They been secretly plotting as though I was Ken Lotan I'm
still holding the grown they don't like the way it sounds*

*Call me the evil villain the one who be stealing your career
aspirations bury them like a cremation*

**Years have passed while scouring for new talent young
contenders even pretenders just to add to the rap members**

*Internet sensation with a wild occupation Imma put her to
the test no time for wasting Sending tweets an even diss may
have you a little piss that's the chance I'm willing to take to see
if you will bite or eventually break*

New girl and I'm coming the word on the street
I got you running

On site and we're rumblings from them words you be
mumblings next time you'll be tumbling the bag
not fumbling

Say my name I made it in the game I do it for the money not
for the fame bunny rabbit diamond chain

I'm Kat T you don't want to see me like the devil you
better flee in the house safe place to be we all know
you really scared of me

Grammy nominee sorry no apology

Why you mad throwing shoes going for bad hey shoeless or
should I say clueless running up acting like you ready to do this
too bad you missed but Hollie hand you kissed

Got you acting dissolute unplug then mute stuck
on quiet so reboot

waiting for that next hot track drop a line get
feedback rewind then come back

You thought it was that easy cause your songs went
breezy is that what you call teasing me

When they met her thought she was better wrong
move not to clever

Imma keep spitting words like lightning have you
so mesmerized util it's frightening

Time to play catch up mess around get the hiccups
what you say speak up scared of who?

Not you

**Next one came and then unveil let's call her Mane &
Tales** *I wonder how you sound on the ad-libs or
are you just another industry
puppeteer*

I heard you wanted a fight Imma step up to the mic like
Wholyfill and Myke I'm throwing barz not bites

I usually respect all the vets even the ones who act like pets I
don't take kind to senior citizens threats

I'll have you leaking like a diuretic I see your face dripping
soak and wet mess around and need a paramedic

my words are unapologetic I'm young and
energetic your old and pathetic all natural no cosmetic

you talk all that high power shit if I run up bet you do the
splits saying your man be doing hits the only thing he's doing is
taking bitches clits

The icon got played by the con went to the slums just to get
another bum

I heard you was a stupid freak didn't know a trick-a-treat I
laugh at the shit you speak in reality you are super weak

360 isn't what it's cracked up to be the industry is not for the weak no games and fun problem with your relations

What was the sum from 1501 network next to none new location more like slave plantation

Hardesun thought he had a good one a statue of Liberty she isn't pure as you wished her to be

The Baby maybe Cori Canes she didn't claim now you feeling too ashame hot girl summer was looking for a plumber

You thought you could tame the wild animal but her actions and words are not tangible traumasine or should I say drama queen having you walking around like an internet meme

Out one door trying to explore aka nickname industry whore Mane & Tales got a fat oxtail no preservatives just KY gel poisonous lead covered in Ruby Red description read 100% grass feed

Why do you always fight with the other females, are you a mean girl or misunderstood?

Both! Even though I was rised in NY I'm still a caribbean native I feel sometimes like an outsider trying to fit in Meanwhile the rest of society views me as an African American We are spicy and sometimes aggressive fast talking people Some may misconscue our demeanor as being rude and arrogant but that's are traits Our culture is different in many ways Also I'm tired of phony industry people always trying to use me like my feeling or expectations does not matter

How are you and female Nemo? *Being an inspiring artist going from Tic Toc to having a feature with an icon is one thing but competing with record sales at the same time can be frustrating I'm good hopefully she is too*

What title would you give the other female rappers?
OverratedEntertainers

Yellow brick road is what they sold thought I was
sleep then I rose

impersonating me so I've been told all they do is lie Pinoc-
chio turn water into ice now your froze industry trying to
replicate me very bold I'm deep rooted like a cavity mold

it's so sad no originality they act like we don't know hit you
with a double placebo 2 for 1 fake promo

applying pressure you thought Tesla Lambo shire power
can't catch her comedy at the Apollo amateur

Two peas in a pod copycats just stop got you looking
sideways always trying to ride my waves

Why all the fuss left you in the dust industry don't trust hit
records a must

Why all the hate Imma sit next to the greats it's hard to anticipate my next move or your fate

My rap game is topflight rock you to sleep goodnight story time I might learn my words recite

After 1 is 2 first me then you (repeat) bubble gum rappers who unwrapped her? next page new chapter

My name is Lacy but they call me La La
outspoken mean what I say cause I'm woken will let loose
when provoking Fuck granny goose was the words spoken

I tried to keep the peace even called a truce wasn't trying to
do elderly abuse I'm quick with the words hard to swallow blow
up the spot leaving it hollow then hit the unfollow

Your old better retire them hot flashes got you on fire, your
time about to expire Depends is what she require

I committed the forbidden sin blame it on my evil twin got
you hot and bothered don't send for me I'm not your
son or daughter

Now you expose dead it; it's close

Season 1 how did she win it wasn't from the ink pen
it must have been her light skin no need to
rescind we don't need another spin

You had a mentor instead you did a detour now
your career is unsure

your head and mouth is big Imma watch the grave you dig

Side chick chronicles you're so comical 21 karats baby and
marriage what happen to your song let's call it a miscarriage

There is no rap female higher than me even though there's a
variety I'm next to Gawd in society can't change
the barbs reality

You slick with them words I'll have you impaired and slurred
afterwards to many to ignore now it's time to even the score
Chastising me now its own I'm old and tire Bitch Be Gone

Where you shocked after La La released those texts messages and audio? *I wasn't shocked disappointed because I reached out to have a conversation*

Generation Z especially the females are hard to communicate with and they feel entitle

If they are not catty or cussing you out there is little respect Everybody common sense is not common

Is there anyone in the industry you would like to work with? *Let me think about it.......*

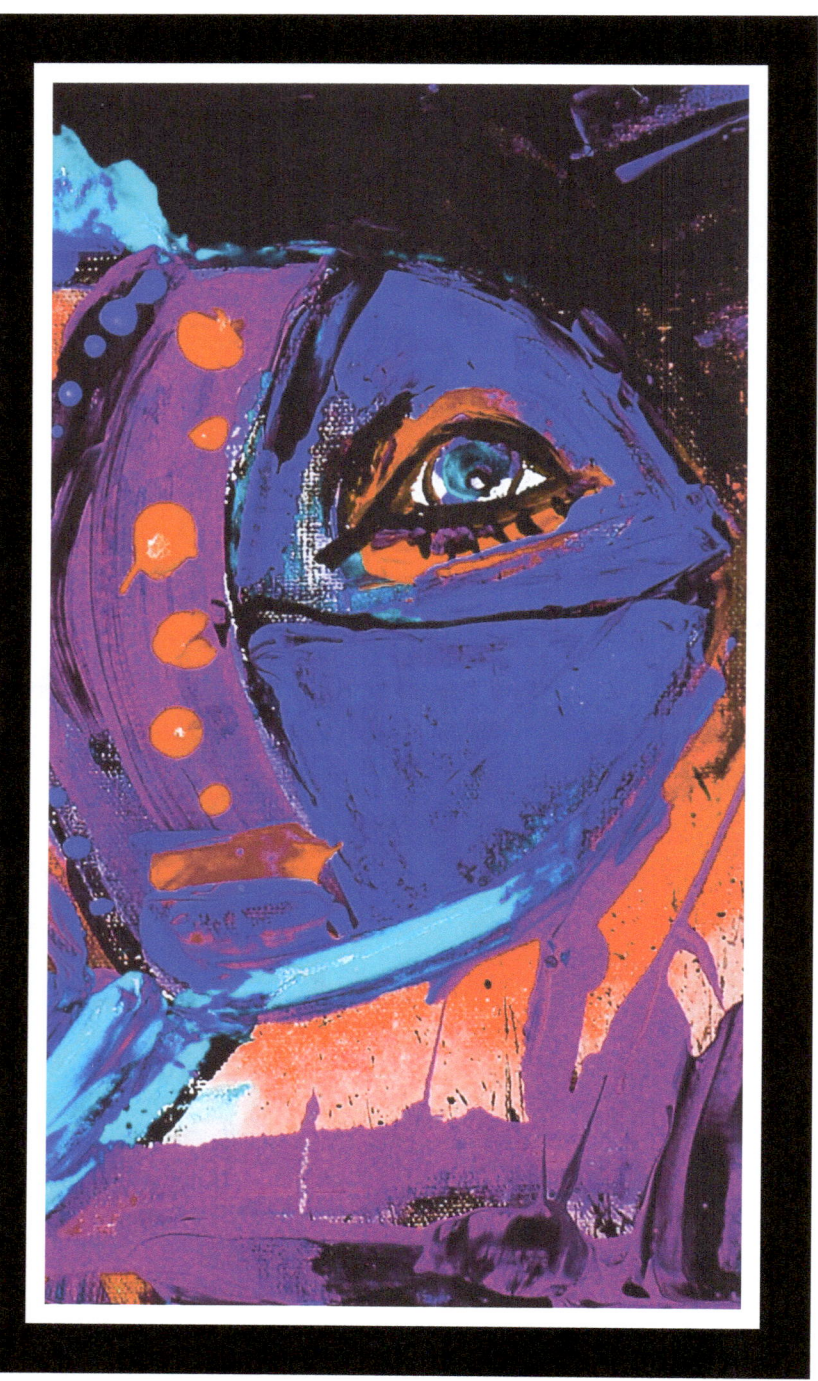

Little fish wish the big head tried to sneak diss but fell instead

you at the bottom trying to get to the top no time for games just Tic Toc

Read the story find the plot next time sit and watch

If Pinky was a boy her name would be Ricky I would have
all yall bitches licking on my dickey

Open wide now swallow your pride have you
sucking down my semen like a sex demon wake up
you're not dreaming body craving like an
attic feigning

head shot perfect spot just another one under my notch

Don't none of yall want to see me from Clownye
Barnaby to the circus pony

My pen game is lethal my words just as equal next
song Ether sequel

I hit you with body blows Claressa make you fall like dominoes
gave over Imma call you Rover your bark is loud my bite is felt
new status champion belt

Imma boss chick stab me in the back then I switch Roman
Revenge got you on needles and pins

won't stop keep the barz flowing like the ocean with no ending
release the hatch cause I'm sending

Next case will end in space obliviated no sound just waste

*1st came the twist next was the diss I got all the opps
lined up on my list*

dumb you wish I just look like this

*lack of talent in the wrist don't know how they still exist
I got you totally piss*

*battling me is a career catastrophe I'll make you change
your whole trajectory*

my music is longevity others just started puberty

I play chess yall play cards yall come weak Imma come hard
hit the button then disregard touch down at the 4th yard

All yall do is run them chops records are playing on flip flop
wrong team; team opps better chance of winning with them slots

I'm team solo Imma come with 4 more hit you like a stinger
favorite candy Butterfinger got 2 more middle finger's

I'm the best just confess now you feeling the
pressure from your successor

you felled the test bow down I suggest get the iron
now you press

all my opps started a protest playtime is over I killed
you all decompress

Are you scared to challenge male rappers? *Not at all! I stay ready for battle rather its existing or a newcoming artist*

Part of me like to test their skills as well as sharpen mines This is the art of war Like most men tough skin should be your next to kin

Who are the movers and shakers? *The only thing moving and shacking is a whole lot of asses*

Do you feel like you're too old to be shacking your arthritis oops I mean ass? *You are only old as you feel but it has crossed my mind*

**Have you given any thought about
retirement?**

*I admit sometimes it's hard to quit I live for this shit It's not
in my anatomy so come with a new strategy*

*Far as for some other people hell yeah they should retire
Bwahahahahaha*

QUEEN

Just call me Vinis and Cerena I'm the queen in this arena
coming through like hurricane Katrina got you bitches on hiatus

I speak facts bitches is fake like wax Keep it a stack
like that gold on them racks Here's my
disclaimer I stay ready like a fully
loaded chamber

The industry tried to get rid of me so they
decided to clone me I question science stem until I saw them

It's starting to get boring until I started roaring like the
alpha female I'm the common denominator do the
math whose the greater

just call me terminator too late to save her
overnight became a traitor shred them all meat grater

Millenniums

New Millennium I hit you with the titanium so tell all you
hellions they sound like comedians

I gas it up with premium while others are
regular who developed her need a fix editor ghost didn't
come close I need a competitor

2023 new movie female Radio too bad to slow can't keep up
just tiptoe welcome to the sideshow

All these pickme cattle are runaway shadows New motto
rainbow hair with apple bottoms Lyrics caused postpartum

time for new hobby it's called making pottery wrong mistake
losing the lottery it's next to living in poverty just call it
a highway robbery near death close artery

TRAPPED

I'm so lyrical have you wishing for a miracle you're
so basic it's typical

can't think it's called mind control walking around looking
like a troll so empty mind and soul your lifeline is so critical

need more favors they came in layers for all you imitators
looking for a savior got you hook up to
respirators

now you have done the unthinkable fallen so deep into the
rabbit hole contract on lock no
loopholes

expressing your voice you thought it was a free choice
running out of time before your outsource

Now you smiling cause you learned a few tricks from Vick
Canyon Wild'n the way you move is like meowing I'm on
standby cause I'm prowling

none of yall have a clue it's starting to be DeJa'Vu take a
lesson out of my course it's a marriage
without a divorce

LEGEND

Some call it a comeback Imma call it a highjack got a lot to unpack aka talking smack

Thursday throwbacks post a pic Kodak silky straight it's called Brazilian Yak

09 Shack spitting them barz Imma piggyback like magazines on discharge causing fires from the smoke taking names and casting votes

I don't do tap dancing I'm freelancing no time for romancing just ask Pope Kansas

from all the drama to my persona I put the period to the comma

I'm convinced these bitches are low key dense like 45 I apply pressure now they tense hate to see me coming got you hackling and humming

Back to the basics I put my flow on it and laced it too good just embrace it mouthwatering you can taste it

15 years in the game I still remain so put some respect on my name

LAST CHANCE

*I heard my name mention so now you got my
attention time served no suspension just call me
Mrs. Lynchpin*

*Final warning no exemptions time to clear your
true intentions*

*I see you broke the silence contract from queen to
copycat a major breach with a severe impact*

*the damage is done we all know who really won It's
sounds like you want a final run cause you
already begun no file no harm I'll have you
praying trying to be reborn*

*Hollywood squares came in pairs many have tried
but only 1 dared*

*Mirror: mirror on the wall who's the fakest of them
all Tattoo, Light Bright, or Too Tall?*

The plane: the plane bitches be eaten off me like gravy train

*Some thought they could make me fall but
bitches left packed like a U-Haul*

GANGSTER

If it ain't Pinky is sounds real fishy Clarissa if you feeling a little
risky got my drink now a bit tipsy R.I.P to the homies
Pock and Ziggy

No time for mean mugging Nino Brown he be thugging hear
those shots cause they muzzling bodies buried keep on shoveling

all you see is Ruby Red the same that runs through your
veins the color I don't claim

should have done a hit and run got caught up from that
erection if you looking for affection next time go
a different direction

just like her girlfriend she was Dennis the Menace cause
she rob men then became a chosen spokesman along came a
black token what's the true motive can't even comprehend potus
got that 45 for protection most Dems want to reject him
ain't no such thing as a fair election

I got that extended sleeve keep living in that make
believe Shot out to my locals 44s on my knuckles real ones like
Blanco remind me of my uncle Capone 1 shot to the dome and ya
gone now your color is 2 tone moving like Casper all alone standing
on my principles right or wrong Imma keep it gangster and it's on

I Declare War

*Princess How can I lose when I'm already chose? is the
new anthem the words they be chanting got Doritos
bitches drinking on Fanta's*

*It's been a minute since I did a flex I'm too high power only
fucking with Nasdaq got my foot on their necks watch them
numbers deposit them checks*

*I blew it up like the atomic bomb had the opps succumb
before another Vietnam and for the rest of my sons got your
tongues stuck on numb*

I'm the one they call entice have you stuck
thinking twice

so hot open up your nostrils have you coughing up
your tonsils now your lymph nodes are swollen
can't talk no vocals

cool you off with some ice no need for assistance I'm suffice

Fresh on the scene got a feature with the queen
she crowned me princess fulfilled my dream bitches
mad because we're the new A-Team

she said she's on top all I hear is a flop when I look back
all I see is a trail mad cause I quickly
propel generating them record sales

The bitch said put it on the floor I'm already through
the door I stay quiet it's called ignore How can I lose with
your advice me and the Queen on a money heist

Hello my name is Natalia K I am a single parent and reside in Southern California. As a young child I always liked rhyming poetry, and would write poems as a hobby. The older I became my interest changed but the love still remained. This book was the start of my journey to becoming an indie writer.

Adobe Stock Images
Cover by Alyssa (Fiverr)
Layout by 562Graphics